SNUG AS A BUG?

happy yak

For my lovely Mum! Thank you for always being there and for supporting my writing adventures x
K.N.

For Dara and Walter
A.W.

First published in 2023 by Happy Yak,
an imprint of The Quarto Group.
1 Triptych Place, 2nd Floor, London,
SE1 9SH, United Kingdom.
T (0)20 7700 6700 F (0)20 7700 8066
www.quarto.com

A catalogue record for this book is available from the British Library.

ISBN: 978 0 7112 7484 6

9 8 7 6 5 4 3 2

Manufactured in Shanghai, China CC082023.

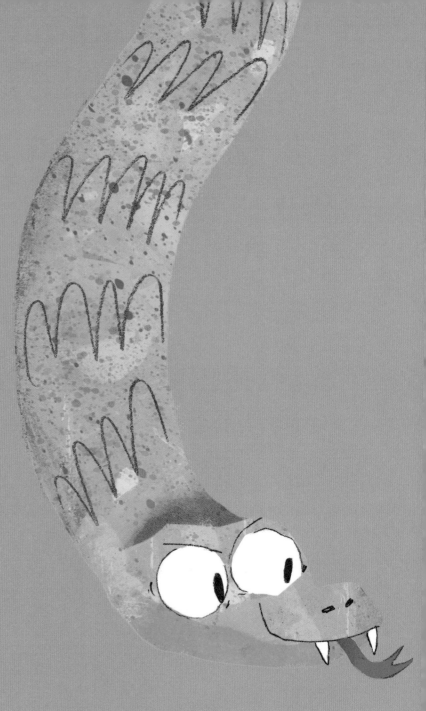

KARL
NEWSON

ALEX
WILLMORE

SNuG
AS A
BuG?

happy yak

I'm as snug as a bug in a rug, I am.

As snug as a bug could be.

There has never been a bug

in **THE WHOLE WIDE WORLD**

so happily snug as me!

Why, **tasty** bug,
it's only me...
It's time for my dinner,
you see.

But I've already *had* my dinner...

My, my, little bug,
aren't you a treat!
You're just in time
for a bite to eat...

No, thank you,
I've already eaten!

I'm as snug as a bug in a rug, I am.
As snug as a bug could be.
There has never been a bug
IN A CAVE OF
CERTAIN DEATH
so happily snug
as me!

Hello there!
Is this...

Oh dear!

I'm as snug as a bug in a rug, I am.
As snug as a bug could be.
There has never been a bug
IN A FOREST OF DOOM
so happily snug as me!

Aha! Somewhere safe to rest my legs and catch my breath and...

WHY DOES THIS

KEEP HAPPENING

TO ME?

I'M AS SNUG AS A BUG IN A RUG, I AM! AS SNUG AS A BUG COULD BE. THERE HAS NEVER BEEN A BUG FLYING... FALLING... FLAPPING! SO HAPPILY SNUG AS MEEEE!

Why did I answer the door?

Greetings bug!
How nice of you to drop by!

Nice to eat you, too.
WHAT?!

Nice.

To.

Eat.

You!

Wait.

What's that sound?

I'm as snug
as a bug in a rug, I am.

As snug as a bug could

be.

Hello bug...

I AM **NOT** FOR **EATING!!**

OH FIDDLESTICKS!

There has never been a bug

IN A CROCODILE'S
BUBBLE-POPPING-REALLY-SMELLY BELLY
so happily snug as me.

I outran a
SLURPING SNAKE.

I escaped
A CAVE OF CERTAIN DEATH.

I trekked through
A FOREST OF DOOM.

I flew
ON THE BACK OF A BIRD.

I sailed a
LEAF OVER A WATERFALL.

And I am NOT snug here.
NOT AT ALL.

You ate the *wrong* bug!

I'M
GOING
HOME!

I may be small...
but I'm *mighty!*

And I've got somewhere
else to be...

...somewhere snug!

Ahem.

Not today, snake.
Not today!

I'm as snug as a bug in a rug, I am.
As snug as a bug could—

DING-
DONG!

Nope.
GO BUG SOMEONE ELSE!
There has never been a bug
IN THE WHOLE WIDE WORLD
so happily snug as me.